ABW
NSV

First published in Switzerland under
the title *Der reiche Mann und der Schuster*.

First published in the United States, Great Britain,
Canada, Australia, and New Zealand in 2002 by
North-South Books, an imprint of Nord-Süd Verlag AG,
Gossau Zürich, Switzerland.

Distributed in the United States by
North-South Books Inc., New York.

Library of Congress Cataloging-in-Publication
Data is available.
A CIP catalogue record for this book is available
from The British Library.
ISBN 0-7358-1675-1 (trade edition)
10 9 8 7 6 5 4 3 2 1
ISBN 0-7358-1676-X (library edition)
10 9 8 7 6 5 4 3 2 1
Printed in Belgium

For more information about our books, and
the authors and artists who create them,
visit our web site: www.northsouth.com

The Rich Man and the Shoemaker

A fable by La Fontaine

Retold and illustrated by Bernadette Watts

NORTH-SOUTH BOOKS
New York / London

There once lived, in a very fine city, a shoemaker who sang happily at his work from dawn till dusk.

Across the street from the shoemaker lived a merchant, so rich he rolled in gold. The merchant never sang and slept little, spending every waking hour counting his riches. He was woken up very early by the shoemaker's happy songs, and during the day he would lose count of his calculations, distracted by the singing.

At last he asked the shoemaker to call at his house. "How much do you earn?" he asked the shoemaker.

The shoemaker laughed and shrugged his shoulders. "I struggle each day to earn enough to put food on the table, and little else," he replied.

"I will give you enough gold to put a feast on your table and more for your wife to store. But you must stop singing!" said the merchant.

The shoemaker was shocked and would not agree to such an arrangement. "We can manage very well without your gold, thank you," he said and went home.

The shoemaker went on singing while he worked, and the merchant became more and more irritated.

One day the merchant called at the shoemaker's shop. The shoemaker was delighted, thinking the rich man had come to order a pair of winter boots, and he sprang up to welcome him.

"You must stop singing, so I can count my gold and get some sleep!" said the merchant. "In return here is a purse full of gold pieces for you. You can take a break from your work. Have some easy days."

"But what would I do without my work?" asked the shoemaker in great surprise. "And as for singing . . . why, if I did not sing, I could not work."

So the merchant left and went back to his own cold and lonely home.

Some time later the merchant called on the shoemaker again. The snow lay thick on the street and across the rooftops. The merchant wrapped himself in a rich cloak and hurried across the street.

"Come in!" called the shoemaker. "Don't stand out there in the bitter cold!"

So the merchant stepped into the warm room. "I will give you all the gold you can ever spend and precious stones, too, if only you will stop singing!" And so saying, the merchant took out a chest inlaid with jewels.

The shoemaker was amazed—he had never seen such riches. It is cold, so cold, he thought to himself. With this gold I could buy my wife and children warm coats, scarves, too. And surely there is enough to buy a roast turkey to put on the table, and more coal to put on the fire.

So he agreed with the merchant to take the gold and stop singing.

The merchant, happy for once, hurried home.

Until I have time to go shopping I must hide these riches, thought the shoemaker. He went out into their little garden and dug a hole, which was difficult as the ground was frozen. There he buried the chest.

The disturbed place in the garden was very easily seen. All night the shoemaker could not sleep, but kept looking out the window. The next day he was too anxious to do any work. Night after night he kept watch on the garden, and day after day he was quiet and worried and unable to work.

If the cat by the fire stretched, the shoemaker thought he heard robbers. He thought that the ticking of the clock was someone sneaking around the house. And when his wife drew water, he believed he heard robbers dragging the chest from the ground. Even his children had to tiptoe about and whisper, so they didn't alarm their poor father.

Then one morning the shoemaker's wife said, "Give back the gold. What has it brought except unhappiness?"

So the shoemaker dug up the chest. He carried it across the street and knocked loudly at the rich man's door.

"Give me back my songs and peaceful sleep!" he said. "Here, take your gold and precious gems."

And the shoemaker returned home to his family,
a happy man again.

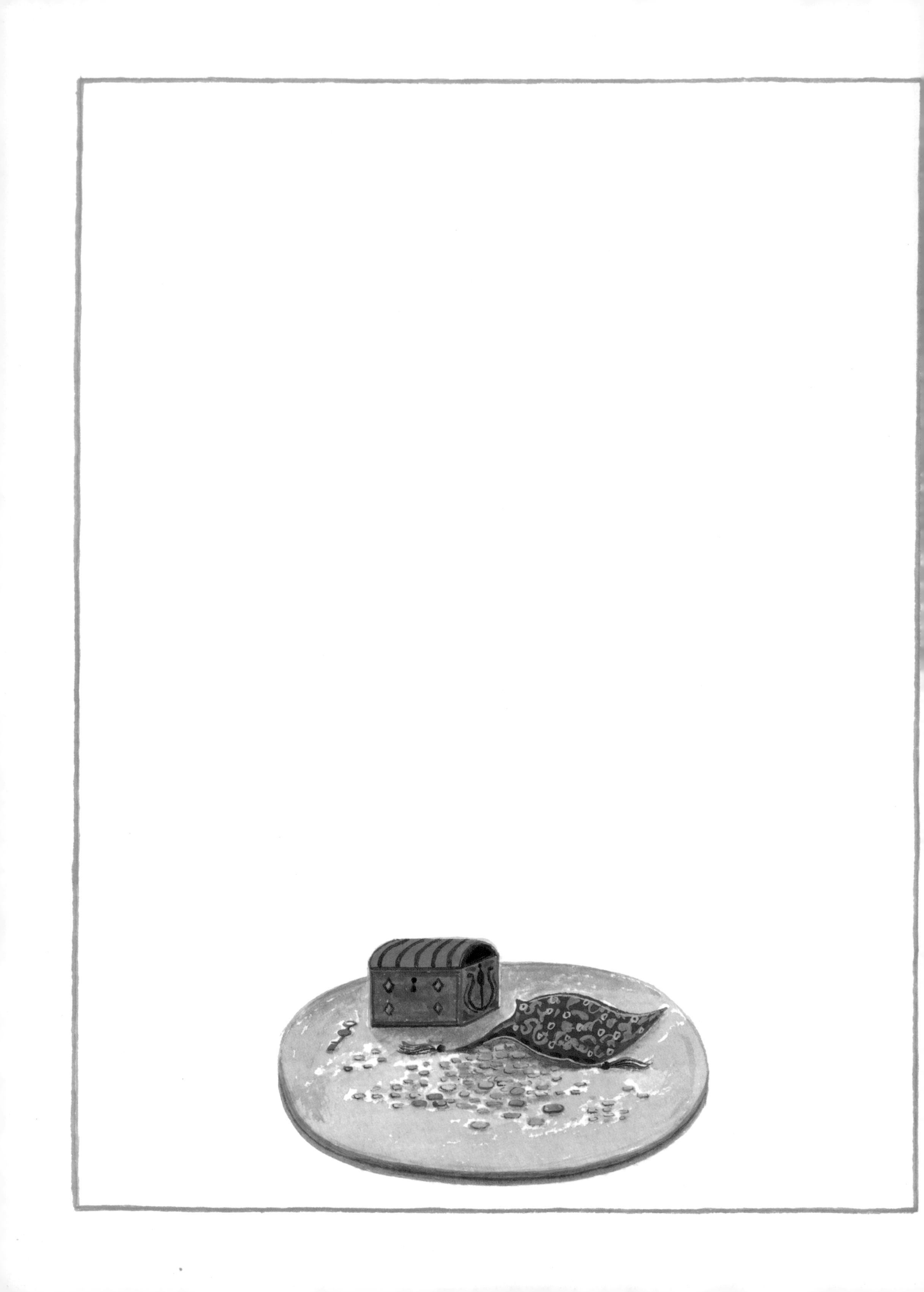

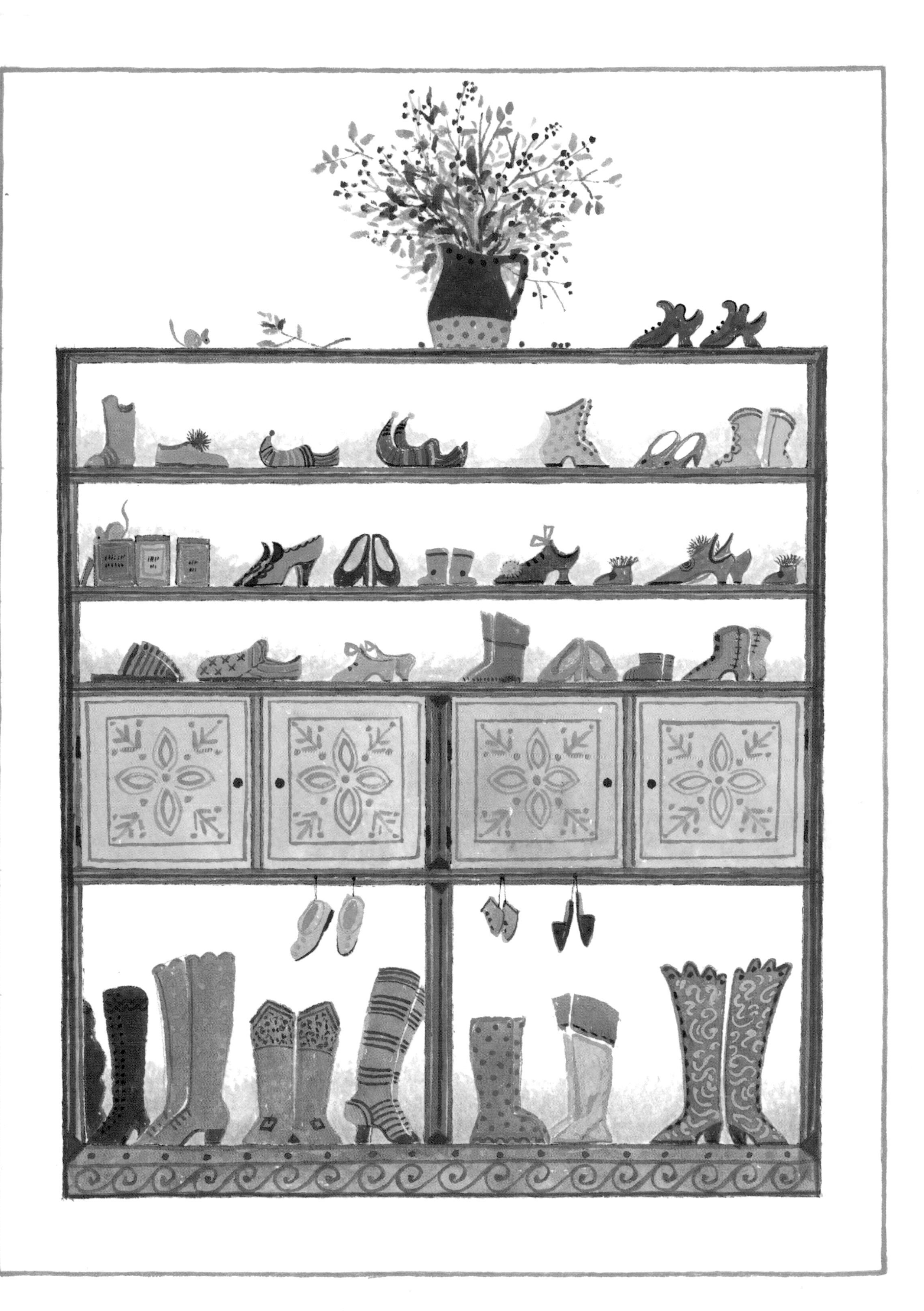